You're Really a Model Now!

by Marcie Anderson

Cover photo by Bichsel Morris
Photographic Illustrators

Published by Willowisp Press, Inc.
401 E. Wilson Bridge Road, Worthington, Ohio 43085

Printed in the United States of America

10 9 8 7 6 5 4 3 2

ISBN 0-87406-042-7

One

"OVER here, Jill! Give us a smile!" Jill Larson flashed a nervous smile at the photographer calling to her.

"We have the mini-cam ready over here, Miss Larson," the pretty reporter from Channel 10 said. "If you'll step this way?"

"Mom? Does my hair look okay?" Jill smoothed her straight blonde hair.

"Fine, honey," Mrs. Larson said, giving her daughter a push. "Go on, they're waiting."

The reporter told Jill to stand in front of a sign reading "Flight 87—New York."

"Ready?" she asked Jill with a smile. "Just relax and be natural."

A cameraman focused the small television camera he held on his shoulder. "Tape rolling. Take one."

"We're at Sea-Tac International Airport today to talk with Jill Larson of Alderwood. She is this year's winner of the *Fashion Miss* magazine's Face of the Future contest. Jill, can you tell us exactly what you've won?"

3

"Well," Jill gulped and tried to smile brightly. "My mom and I are on our way to New York for a week with all expenses paid. I'll have a makeover at the magazine and then be photographed for a summer issue."

"How do you feel about winning this contest?" the reported asked.

"Oh, very excited!" Jill brushed her hair back from her face. "I think it will be really fun to see New York."

"Do you hope to make a career of modeling?"

"I . . . well, I'm not sure yet," Jill answered. "It's too soon to tell."

"I understand you're only thirteen."

"Yes, I'm in the eighth grade," Jill said.

"Good luck in New York, Jill. Your friends in Seattle will be rooting for you! This is Catherine Long for Channel 10 Action News."

"Yea!" Jill's friends and family had gathered behind the TV crew. As soon as the interview was finished they broke into cheers and applause.

"Don't forget us!" Jill's best friend, Becky, called out.

"Silly," Jill said as she gave Becky a quick hug. "I'm only going for a week."

"Be on the lookout for movie stars, okay?" Becky said.

"Jill, they're getting ready to board," her

mom said. "Come on over to the gate now."

It's finally time to go, Jill thought, and I didn't get to say good-bye to Steve. Why isn't he here to see me off? He promised he would be here. Oh, I'm so nervous, she thought. What if I'm not pretty enough and they send me home?

"Bye, Jill. Good luck." Her older brother, Chris, hugged her quickly.

"Have a great time, honey." Jill's father gave her a bear hug. "Here's twenty dollars extra in case you need it. Be careful now," he said. He turned to Jill's mom and hugged her. "See you next week. We'll miss you both."

Jill looked around the airport waiting area anxiously. Where was Steve? He'd promised to come and say good-bye.

"Jill, over here!" Steve called. He was behind a rope near the boarding gate.

Jill ran over to him quickly. "I was afraid you weren't coming," she said.

"I had to wait for my brother to drive me. Here, these are for you." Steve held out a little basket of dried flowers.

"Oh, Steve! How sweet of you." Jill kissed him quickly on the cheek.

"Jill, let's go!" her mom called.

"Bye, Steve." Jill gave him a quick hug.

"Don't let them change you," Steve said. But Jill had turned away and didn't hear.

Jill and her mom grabbed their coats and carry-on bags and hurried to find their seats. "Here, you take the window seat, Jill," Mrs. Larson said. "Maybe we'll see the mountains on our way out."

Jill had flown to Oregon a couple of times to visit her grandparents. But this was her first cross-country flight and her first trip in such a big plane.

"Mom, there must be hundreds of people on this plane. Oh, I almost forgot. Look what Steve gave me as a going-away present." She held up the little basket of flowers.

"He does seem like a thoughtful young man," Mrs. Larson said as she picked up the airline magazine. "I'm glad you've found such a nice boyfriend."

Jill closed her eyes and put her head back. Steve *was* thoughtful . . . and smart . . . and cute. Half the girls in Alderwood Junior High School thought so, too. Steve had been her boyfriend since the beginning of the school year. Jill thought she was lucky that a ninth grader like Steve would have an eighth grader as a girl friend. But Steve told her at least once a week that she was the prettiest girl in the school.

Jill didn't really believe that. She thought she looked too ordinary, too much like the girl next door. There were other girls in her school she thought were prettier, ones who looked older and more mature. And I could lose a little weight, too, Jill thought. It's so hard to keep my weight down when I'm so tall. She hated being one of the tallest girls in her class.

It had just been a joke when she and Becky sent in their school photos to the *Fashion Miss* annual Face of the Future contest. Jill wanted to win the makeover so she'd look a little older. She had told Becky, "I can't look like a kid forever!"

Jill had been so surprised last summer when the magazine wrote back that she was one of fifty semi-finalists. She'd had to send more pictures. Then in November *Fashion Miss* called to say she was one of ten finalists. A week later one of their editors and a photographer arrived to interview Jill and to take lots of photos.

The first weeks of December seemed the longest of Jill's life as she waited to see if she'd won the contest. It was her best Christmas present ever when *Fashion Miss* called to say "Congratulations! We'll see you in New York next month."

The three weeks following Christmas had rushed by in a blur. Jill had to make arrangements to miss school for a week and skip play practice. But now she had all her school books and assignments packed away in

7

her suitcase for the trip. Jill's mother was able to take a week's vacation from her job.

"Are you excited, honey?" Linda Larson asked, squeezing her daughter's arm. "I certainly am! I can't wait to see New York again after all these years."

"I'm kind of nervous about what New York will be like," Jill said. She looked out the window and watched the baggage being loaded.

"Oh, it'll be great!" her mom said. "Remember what the editor told us—parties, a Broadway show, a tour of the city in the *Fashion Miss* limousine. You'll love it. And I'll be there with you every step of the way."

"It sure will be different than Alderwood, won't it, Mom?" Jill smiled as she thought of the two streets in the business section of their little town.

"I should say so," her mom said with a grin. "Alderwood is a nice little town, and I'm glad you and Chris are growing up there. We're lucky to have all the advantages of Seattle nearby, too. But New York! Well, this is the big time, Jill."

Jill felt butterflies dancing in her stomach as the plane started down the runway. Everyone seemed to be counting on her, yet she didn't really know what to expect. She's never been a model before, although people were always telling her she should be. "You have such a pretty face," people would say. She'd heard it hundreds of times.

"Good morning, ladies and gentlemen, and welcome to Western Airlines Flight 87, direct nonstop jumbo jet service from Seattle to New York's Kennedy Airport."

Jill settled into her seat as the flight attendants demonstrated the oxygen masks. In front of them was a beautiful dark-haired flight attendant, with perfect hair and makeup. "Now, if I looked like that, I wouldn't be so nervous about modeling," Jill said to herself. "She's so polished and . . . sophisticated." That was the right word, and the way Jill wanted to look.

The pilot came on the loudspeaker to say that Mt. Rainier was coming up on Jill's side of the plane.

"Oh, look, Mom, there it is!" Jill cried as Mt. Rainier's majestic peak came into view. "There's nothing else like it, is there? Remember when we drove up there last summer?"

"But honey, you've seen Rainier all your life. Now you're going to see the heart of the fashion industry, the heart of the whole country, really."

"I can't wait, Mom."

"This is it, honey! We'll go for it together!"

Two

"EXCUSE me, are you Jill Larson?" Jill looked up at the pretty dark-haired flight attendant she had admired at the beginning of their flight. Jill nodded.

"And you're Mrs. Larson? I'm Jane Cooper. *Fashion Miss* notified the airline you'd be aboard today. Congratulations on winning the contest!"

"Oh, thank you." Jill smiled shyly at Jane.

"I used to model in New York before I started flying," Jane said. "I think you'll really enjoy it."

"This is Jill's first experience with modeling," her mother said. "I think she's a little nervous."

"This is your first flight to New York then?" Jane asked. "Jill, would you like to come up front and meet the pilots? The cockpit is really interesting if you've never seen it before."

Jill followed Jane to the front of the huge

plane. Jane introduced her to several other flight attendants as "the new *Fashion Miss* model." Jill held her chin a little higher as the flight attendants gave her their congratulations and best wishes. Maybe after her makeover she'd look as sophisticated as they did.

Jill was introduced to the pilots. She got a quick glimpse of huge panels of flight instruments.

"*Fashion Miss* magazine?" one of the pilots said. "My daughters read that cover to cover every month. And they enter those contests every year. I'll be sure to tell them I met this year's winner."

"Doesn't she have a pretty face?" Jane remarked to the pilots as she turned to leave the cockpit. "I know she'll be a success in New York."

Jane paused after the door to the cockpit closed and locked automatically. "It's a good thing you're getting started in modeling so young. They say it's best to get established with a top agency while you're still in your teens."

"I do have some agency interviews set up in New York," Jill said. "But we're coming back home after just a week. I have to get back to school."

"Well, give it a chance if you can," Jane

said. "You're only young once."

Jill thanked Jane for the tour and returned to her seat. Did girls her age really live in New York and model fulltime? she wondered. But that was out of the question for her. She had to get back to school and her mom had to return to her job as a surgical nurse. Jill's friends were expecting her back in only a week. So were Dad and Chris . . . and Steve. She could never stay in New York.

Jill spent most of her time on the flight rereading the past three issues of *Fashion Miss*. This time she looked at every model carefully, studying each girl's hairstyle and makeup. She noticed what the models did with their hands, how their eyes looked, how they stood. I have so much to learn, she thought. I wish I'd modeled before and then I wouldn't feel like such a beginner.

By the time they reached New York, Jill and her mom were exhausted, but excited, too. Jill was amazed at the sight of New York at night. "It goes on forever," she said.

"No, it just seems that way," her mom answered. "But it truly is a big city, a different world than Seattle."

Jill's mom had their suitcases loaded into a taxi and they went straight to their hotel.

"There's so much traffic," Jill said. "And why do the taxis honk at each other so much?"

Her mother laughed. "This is New York, Jill. That's the lifestyle here. It's push, push push in Manhattan—that's where we are, the downtown part of New York City."

The lobby of their hotel was huge, with a great crystal chandelier and burgundy carpet. Jill followed her mom and the bellman to their room in a daze. I'm so tired, she thought. I haven't done anything but sit on a plane all day, but I'm exhausted anyway. A long shower and some hot food, that's what I want.

"Just look at this, Jill," her mother said. "Flowers for us from the magazine!"

"And here's a fruit basket and champagne, Mom," Jill said. "They really go all out at *Fashion Miss,* don't they?" Jill flopped down on one of the king-sized beds.

"Yes, this is room 1021," she heard her mother on the telephone. "I'd like two shrimp salads and a pot of tea, please. About how long? Thank you."

"Shrimp salad! Mom, I'd rather have a hamburger and fries. I want something good for dinner. I'm starved."

"You have to get used to eating lightly, Jill. You're a model now, don't forget." Mrs. Larson opened a suitcase and began to unpack.

Everything's different here, Jill thought as she got up to unpack her own clothes. And I'm not sure I'm going to like it.

But the next day Jill thought New York looked better. Their hotel room was beautiful, with a sunken tub in the bathroom and a sweeping view of the city. They had a quick breakfast in their room and then were picked up by the *Fashion Miss* limousine. It was a crispy-cold, sunny day and Jill thought that must be a good sign. It was certainly a nice change from Seattle's rainy winters.

The limousine driver opened their doors in front of a huge modern building on a busy street. "Here you are, ladies," he said as he helped them out of the car. *"Fashion Miss* headquarters are on the tenth floor."

Jill's stomach quaked and her mouth was dry as they rode the elevator. What would they say to her? Would everyone be glad to see her? Or would they treat her like just a kid from the sticks?

"Are you sure I look okay, Mom?" Jill asked. She had struggled for an hour the night before trying to decide what to wear. She had settled on tailored black pants and a light pink sweater. "Maybe I look too young in this pink color?

"You look just fine honey. They want you to look fresh and young. That's the whole idea of the contest," said Mrs. Larson. She gave Jill's shoulder a squeeze as the elevator doors slid open. Jill smiled at her mom.

They stepped into an elegant lobby with gray carpet, peach-colored sofas, and tall green plants.

"Good morning," an attractive blonde receptionist said. "Are you Jill Larson and Mrs. Larson? Right this way, please. Ms. Paget is expecting you."

"Jill! I'm so glad to meet you." A tall, thin woman with very short, dark hair stood up from her chair and shook their hands.

"And Mrs. Larson—welcome to *Fashion Miss*. I'm Natalie Paget, editorial director. We're very pleased to meet you at last."

Jill and her mother sat in leather chairs across from Ms. Paget. Jill tried not to stare at Natalie Paget's outfit. She was wearing a dark purple dress and a huge gold necklace that looked like a collar. The necklace was trimmed with peacock feathers. Jill smiled when she thought what her friends would think of that getup. Peacock feathers!

Natalie Paget showed them their schedule for the week. Jill stared at her copy. They were busy every minute of the week! Makeup, hairstyling, shopping, a tour of the city, modeling agency interviews, photo sessions— everything was planned out for her.

"This is going to be such a fabulous opportunity for you, Jill," Natalie said.

"Modeling can do so much for you, personally as well as financially. We've had several cover girls here who have gone on to TV and the movies. The sky's the limit, really!" She smiled brightly at both of them.

"I know your schedule is a bit overwhelming, but since you'll be here such a short time . . . well, that's the only way we can fit it all in," Natalie said. "Now I'm going to turn you over to my assistant, Katie Callard. Katie will be escorting you most of this week. She'll introduce you to the other editors—the people in charge of each department of the magazine. And she will be in charge of your makeover this afternoon, too."

Jill liked Katie right away. She seemed very friendly and energetic. Jill's first appointment was a fitting for her fashion layout in the magazine. Then she had to stand quietly with her arms stretched out while the fashion editor and her assistant pinned the dozens of clothes to fit. They pinned the clothes in back so it looked like they fit Jill perfectly.

"Are you going to sew the clothes so they'll really fit me?" Jill asked.

"Oh, no," one of the editors laughed. "We just make everything *look* like it fits."

Next Jill was photographed in the small *Fashion Miss* studio for her "before" photos. Katie added a little makeup and rearranged

Jill's hair for some of the photos. "We don't want you to look too polished for these pictures," Katie explained. "Then you'll look really great after your makeover."

After a quick lunch Jill, her mom, the photographer, and Katie went to Mr. Kevin's Salon for Jill's hairstyling. Mr. Kevin was a tall, bald man dressed in a black jumpsuit. Jill was very nervous about having such a famous hairdresser work on her hair. What if he wanted to cut it all off in some strange New York style?

"Such a pretty face," he said. "But too much hair! It's hiding those great cheekbones. And your bangs have to be shorter to open up your eyes. You'll definitely be cover girl material with shorter hair."

But I like my hair shoulder length, Jill thought. Her hands grabbed her long blonde hair protectively.

"Jill, Natalie and I both think a shorter cut will be much more versatile," Katie said. "You'll be able to look much older in photos when you need to. Mr. Kevin is the best, Jill. You can trust his judgment."

"Mom?"

"You can always let it grow back," Mrs. Larson said. "Why don't you try it?"

So Jill let Mr. Kevin cut her hair in a layered style with short, feathery bangs. The photographer captured every snip on film.

"You see," Mr. Kevin said as he styled her hair with a curling iron. "Now you can look sixteen or even twenty with the right makeup. Or you can still look like a sweet young girl with simple makeup and styling." He turned Jill so she could see her new hairstyle in the triple mirror.

"I do look older!" Jill exclaimed. "You're right, Mr. Kevin."

"Now, we have to hurry back to our studio," Katie said. "We have the makeup artist waiting to do your 'after' photos. It'll be a new you, Jill!"

Jill couldn't believe it when she saw herself in the mirror when the makeup lady had finished. "Who is this girl?" she asked herself.

The makeup artist had used more makeup than Jill usually wore. My eyes look huge, Jill thought. And I look older and . . . maybe even a little glamorous. Jill turned her head to see herself better in the mirror. Click, click, click. The photographer was shooting away constantly.

Jill smiled and her eyes sparkled. I wish I always looked this nice, she thought.

"That's great, Jill," the photographer said. "Now turn this way. And tilt your head to your left . . . more. That's fine. You're doing well for a beginner."

The fashion editor brought Jill some different clothes to wear for more "after" pictures. "We like to have a variety of shots for the 'after' poses," she explained.

Jill was photographed in a plaid shirt and then in a beautiful lace blouse. "Here, Jill," Katie said. "Try holding these roses against the lace."

"Excellent!" the photographer said. "You have a very romantic expression, Jill. Are you thinking of your boyfriend back home?"

"Well, no," Jill smiled. "Actually I wasn't. I was thinking about how much I like my new look." She looked down at the roses and smiled. Click, click, click.

"Perfect!" Katie cried. "Very sweet, but not too innocent. You have more style now, Jill. You're not just the girl next door anymore. You're really a model now!"

Three

"DAD! It's great to hear your voice. How's everything going?"

"You're a star, honey! Everyone we know within fifty miles saw you on Channel 10 Sunday night. And just wait till you see the article in today's paper."

"Save it for me, okay, Dad?" Jill asked.

"Of course, honey. I bought ten extra papers so you'll have lots of copies for your scrapbook. How's it going out there?"

"Great, Dad. I had my makeover yesterday and I really think I turned out well."

"Makeover?" Chuck Larson's voice was doubtful. "You were perfect the way you were."

"Well this is my New York look," Jill tried to explain. "That was part of winning the contest remember?"

"Just don't let them make you look too old," her father cautioned. "You're still only thirteen years old, Jill."

"Here's Mom," Jill said. "See you on Sunday."

I'll always be a little girl in my dad's eyes, she thought as she got ready for bed. He never wants me to do anything grown-up.

She had felt very grown-up earlier that night and not like just a pretty little girl. Natalie Paget had taken them to an elegant restaurant to welcome them to New York. Jill had tried her first lobster and even ordered a special flaming dessert.

"Just because today is so special," her mom had said when Jill ordered the rich dessert. "It's the beginning of a new life for you, Jill."

Natalie had smiled and had lifted her glass in a toast. "To Jill—our newest Face of the Future, and perhaps the next toast of New York. You just may have what it takes, Jill, if you want it enough."

Jill wasn't sure what Natalie meant. But she knew she was beginning to enjoy New York. She liked riding in the *Fashion Miss* limousine, having everyone tell her she was beautiful and a natural at modeling, trying new foods like lobster and bagels. Alderwood just can't compete, she thought.

The next day, Tuesday, was even busier than the previous day. In the morning Jill and her mom took a quick tour of the city in the limousine. Katie met them for lunch at a Japanese restaurant and then took them to Jodine's, a huge department store. Jill had won a $400 wardrobe to be selected there as part of the contest.

"I didn't even know about this prize!" Jill said to Katie.

"Jodine's just decided to participate a few weeks ago," Katie said. "I'll help you pick out some of the latest New York fashions, Jill."

"I think I'll buy some things to take home to Dad and Chris while you're shopping," Jill's mom said. "I'll meet you at the main entrance at two."

Katie breezed through the junior department of Jodine's, grabbing clothes off racks and counters for Jill to try on.

"How do you know what I'll like, Katie?" Jill asked.

"Oh, I just know," Katie answered. "You need some 'young model' clothes. More high fashion and a little more sophisticated. More of an uptown look than a hometown look."

Jill tried on all Katie's selections. She had to admit Katie was right. Now Jill felt like she really belonged in New York. She had the right hairstyle, the right makeup, the right clothes. She didn't feel so much like an outsider anymore.

Wonder what Steve would think of my new

look, she thought as she turned slowly in front of the mirror. I'll bet he wouldn't like these improvements.

Jill added a jacket in the new length and stood back to admire the total effect. Dynamite! If Steve couldn't appreciate her new, improved looks, too bad. And anyway, she thought, Steve and Alderwood are about a million miles away.

Katie and Jill made their final selections and rejoined Jill's mother. "Mom, wait till you see the great clothes we found," Jill said. "These clothes are way ahead of what they're wearing back in Alderwood. The styles are so advanced here."

"You can give me a fashion show when we get back to the hotel," Jill's mother said, smiling at her daughter's enthusiasm.

Katie called a taxi and explained Jill's next appointment. "Here are all the pictures you sent in to *Fashion Miss*. You can keep them with you now. This is one of the top modeling agencies we're going to visit next. If you want to continue modeling you'll have to be accepted by an agency. Then they'll send you on interviews to find modeling jobs."

"But I'll only be here this week," Jill said. "How..."

Her mother cut her off. "Let's just see what they say, Jill. Natalie, Katie, and I want you to see if you can be accepted by an agency. Then we'll decide what to do next."

Her mom gave Jill her famous look that meant, "Don't ask any more questions if you know what's good for you." So Jill didn't say anything else. But she wondered what her mother had meant. And why would they have to "decide what to do next"?

Jill kept thinking about what her mother had said while they were waiting at the agency. She filled out a short application form before she and her mom were called into an inner office.

"Good afternoon, I'm Tanya Thompson, director of new models here." Tanya chatted for a few moments, directing most of her conversation to Jill. "Why do you want to be a model, Jill?"

"Well, people are always telling me I should be," Jill answered. "I'm interested in acting and I'm in our school play right now. Modeling might help me get into acting." Jill wasn't sure if that was a good answer.

"Lots of models do go on to theater or TV," Tanya said. "Did you bring your pictures with you?"

Jill handed over the envelope of photos Katie had given her.

"Hmmm," Tanya said, as she flipped through the photos. "You do show potential for someone so young. But we have three fairly new blonde girls now, so I'm afraid we won't be able to use you at this time."

Tanya stood up and handed Jill's pictures back. "Do try the other agencies though. And good luck to you."

Katie was waiting for them in the lobby. "Any luck?"

"No. And it was over so fast. She hardly talked to me at all." Jill shoved her arms into her coat sleeves.

"Don't be discouraged so soon," Katie said. "There are three more top agencies and then some very good smaller ones we want you to try. In fact we're on our way to another of the big agencies right now."

The next interview went about the same, except this time there were four other girls waiting in the lobby ahead of Jill. Each one went in the interviewer's office and then came out after only a few minutes.

"See, Jill," her mom whispered. "You're not the only one."

Jill's interview was very short and the man barely glanced at her photos. He gave her the same advice. "Try the other agencies."

Katie said that those words were actually encouraging. "If you didn't have any potential, they wouldn't tell you that," she said.

"Do you think I have what it takes to be a

model?" Jill asked, quietly.

"You won our contest!" Katie said, smiling. "You're pretty enough, tall enough, almost thin enough. It just depends on how hard you're willing to work at it, on how much you want to be a model."

"I sure want to try it," Jill said. "What's on our agenda for tonight? Is tonight the Broadway play?"

They went back to their hotel to rest before dinner and the theater. Jill was hoping there might be a letter from Steve waiting for her. But then she realized a letter couldn't have reached her so soon. It already seems like I've been here for weeks, she thought, instead of only three days.

Jill looked at the basket of dried flowers Steve had given her. It sat on the nightstand next to her bed. What a sweetheart, she thought as she closed her eyes to rest. But I don't think he'd like New York. . . .

The play that night was wonderful—a new musical. The girl who played the lead wasn't much older than Jill. Maybe if I did stay in New York, Jill thought, and took lots of acting lessons, I could be up on stage like that.

She hummed the theme song from the musical all the way back to their hotel. "Maybe I should take singing lessons, Mom," Jill said.

Mrs. Larson smiled at her daughter in a knowing way. "It's catching, isn't it?"

"What is?" Jill asked.

"The magic of Broadway."

Four

THE next morning Jill had two agency interviews. One was disappointing and over quickly. But the second interview went on for over half an hour and Jill was encouraged.

The interviewer, Mrs. Ballenger, looked at Jill's photos carefully and then measured Jill's height. "Five six—that's great for your age. You're probably still growing." She had Jill step onto a scale. "Let's see . . . a hundred and fifteen. You'd have to lose five pounds or so. How are you at dieting?"

"Okay," Jill said hesitantly. She'd never had to diet before.

"I'll have to speak with our agency owner. Could you wait just a moment?" Mrs. Ballenger took Jill's photos and left the room.

"Jill, they're interested in you," her mother whispered. "This could be it!"

"But Mom, we can't stay here in New York! Dad wouldn't let us anyway, even if we wanted to. He'd want us to come home."

"You leave your father to me," her mother said as the interviewer came back into the room.

"I'm so sorry," Mrs. Ballenger said kindly. "Our owner feels we've taken on enough new girls of your type recently. But we would like you to check back with us later if you're still interested—say in a year or two."

"Thank you," Jill said numbly as she got up to leave.

"Have you tried the Prestige Agency yet?" Mrs. Ballenger asked. "They're a bit smaller and rather new, but they're very good with young teenagers."

"We see them on Friday," Jill's mom said.

"A friend of mine is an interviewer there," Mrs. Ballenger said. "I'll give her a call for you if you'd like."

Jill thanked her for her interest.

"Don't give up just yet, Jill," Mrs. Ballenger said. "Sometimes it takes a lot of looking to find the right agency."

* * * * * *

Natalie Paget met Jill and her mother at *Fashion Miss* headquarters and took them to a fancy Italian restaurant for lunch. Then they hurried back to *Fashion Miss* to prepare for

Jill's fashion photo session.

Katie explained everything about the photo session to Jill. "This is called a shoot, because we're shooting pictures, not you," she joked. "And we're doing the pictures outside and in some special buildings. That's called 'on location'. Glen is the photographer, Jason is the hairstylist, Marta is the makeup artist and Karen is the fashion stylist. She's in charge of the clothes and accessories."

"That's so many people to remember. Am I the only model for this session?" Jill asked.

"You should see a quad shoot," Katie said. "That's four models being photographed together. Then things really get complicated!" Katie smiled encouragement at Jill. "Don't be nervous. You're going to be just fine. Glen's a great photographer and you're very natural. Just be relaxed."

Jill sat in front of a big lighted mirror while her makeup was being done. She was amazed at the contents of Marta's huge collection of makeup. Marta was obviously a whiz at her profession of makeup artist. She made Jill look natural, but polished, too.

The hairstylist gave Jill's hair a quick set with hot rollers. Jason smiled at Jill as he expertly styled her hair. "You have the look of a winner now, Jill. You can make it big in this business if you try!" Next the fashion stylist gave Jill her first outfit and made sure the clothes fit, at least from the front.

Jill's first photos were in front of the *Fashion Miss* headquarters' sign. Katie explained that the location photos would show Jill in a variety of New York City tourist spots. The whole crew piled into a *Fashion Miss* van and took off on a whirlwind tour of New York. They stopped at Central Park, Greenwich Village, and the World Trade Center, and a New York deli. Jill had to change clothes quickly in bathrooms and twice in the back of the van. She was embarrassed, but no one else was bothered at all.

Katie and Glen told Jill how to pose for each shot. Sometimes she was moving or turning or walking. At the deli she was photographed eating a bagel and cream cheese. She ate two bagels while they were shooting.

At six o'clock the shoot was finally over. Since the deli was the last location of the day, everyone stayed for dinner. Jill was fascinated by the deli. You could order anything—any sandwich combination you could think of. Although she had just eaten a bagel, she ordered an egg salad sandwich on an onion roll, her favorite. Her mother looked disapprovingly at Jill's choice, but Jill didn't care. She was exhausted after such a long day and needed some good food. She had a brownie for dessert, too.

When she got back to their hotel, Jill found a message that Steve had called. But when she returned his call there was no answer.

"You can call him back tomorrow night," her mom said with a yawn. "We have to get right to bed now. We're due at the photographer's studio at nine tomorrow morning."

"But Mom, I want to stay up so I can call Steve back later. And you know my favorite TV shows are on Wednesday night."

Mrs. Larson looked stern. "Jill, are you forgetting that tomorrow is one of the most important days of your life? They're taking most of your photos for *Fashion Miss* tomorrow. You have to look really wonderful and for that you need your rest."

* * * * *

The next morning Jill and her mother had to get up at six so Jill could wash her hair, do her exercise routine, have breakfast, and be at the studio by nine. All the same people were there to help Jill get ready.

The photographer's studio was different from the small studio at *Fashion Miss*. Glen's studio was the top floor of an old warehouse, with huge windows and white walls. Big sheets of colored paper were taped to the walls in various places. "That's so we can get a plain, colored background," Glen explained.

Jill had her hair and makeup done in a small dressing room. The stylist was laying out each outfit, complete with shoes and accessories.

It's kind of nice to be pampered like this, Jill thought as Jason worked on her hair. All these people are working to make me look good. "I wish they could make me look like this every day," Jill said to herself.

"Okay, Jill, here's your first outfit," the stylist said. She handed Jill a summer dress with high-fashion styling.

I could never wear something like this in Alderwood, Jill thought. My friends would have a great laugh over something this different. But here . . . in New York, Jill decided, this dress would be perfect.

Glen told Jill to stand in front of a gray background. "Now put your hands on your hips," he said. "Maybe one hand in back . . . tilt your chin more. Fine!" His camera clicked away constantly.

Jill changed outfits several times and had her hair and makeup adjusted each time. For each outfit she posed in front of different colored backgrounds.

Soon Jill was enjoying herself. She could move and turn and twirl just like the models she'd seen on TV commercials.

"That's fine, Jill," Glen said. "You're doing a great job for a beginner. Keep moving!" His camera never stopped clicking.

"Isn't this taking an awful lot of film?" Jill asked Glen.

"Film is the cheapest thing in the world," Glen answered. "Ask any art director. We want to have tons of shots to choose from. Lean a little to the right now. And you never want to go back and reshoot!"

Jill changed to a casual jeans outfit next. "I've never seen jeans cut like this," she told the stylist.

"Oh, they're the latest from Italy," Karen, the stylist, said. "They'll be the rage all over the country by next summer when this issue comes out."

"They won't be in Alderwood," Jill said to herself. "These jeans will never make it back there."

Katie burst into the studio with a big smile. "Okay, gang, we're on for this afternoon!"

"What's on?" Jill asked.

"We didn't want to tell you until it was definite," Katie explained. "But it's great news. It can make your career, Jill! This afternoon we're shooting close-ups for the cover of *Fashion Miss!*"

"Close-ups of me?" Jill stumbled over the words. "Did you say for the *cover*?"

"That's right," Katie said. "We had an editorial meeting this morning and saw the proofs from yesterday's shoot. They're great, Jill. You're very photogenic, a natural model, really. So we've decided to use you for our cover of the July issue."

"That's wonderful!" Mrs. Larson said as she hugged her daughter. "What an opportunity!"

"That's right," the photographer agreed. "I know several models whose careers really took off after a cover of an important magazine like *Fashion Miss*. You're on your way now, Jill."

After a quick lunch they returned to Glen's studio to shoot the cover. Jill had her hair and makeup touched up. Then she sat on a tall stool in front of special bright lights.

"We have to get the lighting just right so there won't be any shadows," Glen explained.

For over an hour Jill turned her head and shoulders in various poses while Glen photographed her. He told her just what to do and how much to smile. Several times Glen moved Jill to another background. Twice she changed to a different top and had her makeup and hairstyle adjusted.

Finally Jill thought she couldn't smile another minute. She was thirsty and hot from the bright lights. But she kept thinking of *her* face on the cover of *Fashion Miss* and that kept her going.

"Okay," Glen said at last. "I'm sure we have a cover here somewhere. Nice working with you, Jill. Stick with it. You're a natural in front of the camera."

"Did you hear what the photographer said, Mom?" Jill twirled around in the elevator on their way out. "A natural model!"

"I did hear, honey," her mother said, giving Jill a quick hug. "We have some big decisions to make about your future."

"You mean about going on with modeling?" Jill asked. "Staying here in New York?"

"At least giving it a try," Mrs. Larson said. "We have a lot of details to iron out. But we can worry about that tomorrow. Tonight I'm taking you out to celebrate. We have a cover girl in the family now!"

Five

JILL decided to call Steve after dinner that night. She couldn't wait to tell him about her *Fashion Miss* cover. How would he like having a cover girl as his girl friend? she wondered.

"Don't talk very long," Jill's mom warned. "It will cost us a fortune if you don't keep it short."

Jill dialed Steve's number slowly. Had he missed her? she wondered.

"Hello?"

"Hi, Steve. It's Jill."

"Jill! Hi, how's New York?"

"It's great!" Jill said. "I really like modeling. And guess what? I'm going to be on the cover of *Fashion Miss*."

"Hey, congratulations! We have good news here, too. We won our game yesterday against Woodinville and I scored eighteen points!"

"That's good," Jill said.

"Good? That's the best I've had in weeks! And the high school team won this week, too. Your brother, Chris, scored a couple of points," he finished.

"Steve, I miss you. I have to go now. Mom's making faces at me to get off."

"Okay. Well, hurry home. I'll see you at the airport on Sunday, right?"

"I—I'm not sure." Jill didn't know what to say. "I might be staying in New York a little longer."

"What for?" Steve sounded puzzled. "I thought this contest prize was just for a week."

"I can't explain now," Jill said. "I'll talk to you later. I really miss you."

"Well, I miss you, too. So why don't you just come home?" Obviously Steve doesn't understand, Jill thought.

"I've got to hang up or Mom'll kill me!" she said hurriedly. "Bye, Steve."

"I'll call you tomorrow," he said.

Whew, Jill thought as she hung up the phone. He'll never understand if I stay here. He's too worried about his basketball team to understand. And he doesn't know how important a *Fashion Miss* cover is either. It's a lot more important than a junior high basketball team. After all, I'll be famous all over the whole country, Jill said to herself.

She stretched out on the carpet and started doing sit-ups. She could only do ten without gasping for breath. Boy, am I out of shape, Jill thought and let her mind wander ahead to her future. This cover would lead to another, and then maybe TV commercials after that . . . or even a movie. Who knows? Jill thought. I could even be the next Brooke Shields!

"Mom, I really like it here," Jill said suddenly. "I do want to stay in New York and give modeling a try."

"That's the spirit, honey," her mom said. "We'll talk to the people at *Fashion Miss* tomorrow and see if they can help with the arrangements. And I'll call your dad tonight and tell him."

"I don't think he'll like the idea," Jill said doubtfully.

"Well, it will only be for a month or so, a temporary arrangement," Mrs. Larson said. "If you want to stay after that . . . we'll just have to see."

"But what will Dad—"

"Maybe he'll come out for a few days to see us," her mom said. "You deserve this chance. I don't believe in parents holding children back. Just because we're happy in Alderwood doesn't mean it's right for you forever. I'll handle Dad."

"Okay, Mom, thanks," Jill said and gave her

mother a warm hug.

"I'm behind you a hundred percent," Mrs. Larson said. "I always wished my parents had supported me more when I entered the Miss Alderwood contest in high school. I'll never know how my life might have been different if I'd won."

Jill hurried to get ready for bed and fell asleep immediately. Sometime later she felt herself drifting awake. She could hear her mother's voice talking.

"I disagree, Chuck. We've got to give her this chance . . . Yes, she wants it as much as I do . . . It's not permanent, just for a month or six weeks . . . She's going to be on the cover, remember. She could be a star!"

Jill was wide awake by then. Her mom thought Jill could make it to the top in modeling. But her dad didn't want her even to try. Well, I'll show him what I can do, Jill thought as she snuggled back down under the blanket. I'm not just his little girl anymore. I'm a real New York model now!

The next day Jill was up at six to get ready for her interview at the Prestige Agency. She wanted her makeup and her new hairstyle to look perfect. She was determined that this interview would be a success.

"I feel so much better this time," Jill said in the taxi. "Now I have more of a New York look, don't you think?"

"You do look more confident," her mom agreed. "I'm sure one of the agencies will take you on soon."

Jill felt only a tiny bit nervous as they rode the elevator to the seventeenth floor. She was calm and confident when she met the interviewer. She answered all the same questions about her background and why she wanted to be a model. But this time she could tell about her experience at *Fashion Miss* and show some of the proof photos from the location shoot for the magazine.

"Would you wait here a few moments?" the interviewer said. "I'll have to speak to the owner of our agency."

Jill even remained calm while they waited for the woman to come back. "I just have this feeling, Mom. This is it!" Jill whispered.

The interviewer came back into the room with a bright smile. "Jill and Mrs. Larson, this is Garrison Westcott, the agency owner. We both want to welcome you to the Prestige Agency!"

Jill went through the rest of the morning in an excited daze. Her mom and Mr. Westcott talked about contracts, advances, studio apartments, tutors. Jill stared out the huge window at the Manhattan skyline.

"Look out, New York," she said to herself.

"The new Face of the Future is ready and waiting for fame and fortune!" She daydreamed about all the parties she would attend . . . all the pretty new clothes . . . and all the new guys she'd be meeting when she modeled.

"Jill—" The sound of her mother's voice brought Jill back to the present. "We're going to meet the director of new models now."

"Thank you very much, Mr. Westcott," Jill said as she shook his hand. "I'm looking forward to working with the Prestige Agency."

They moved to another large, modern office to meet Alison Drexel, the director of new models. Jill thought Alison was beautiful and glamorous, and Alison explained she was a former model herself.

"Most girls stay in the business only a few years," Alison said. "Then they move on to other things—acting, college, or jobs like mine."

Alison began to explain the new models division. "We're called the testing board here, because you'll be testing with photographers to build up your portfolio. You'll be modeling for a beginning photographer and then you both can use your photos for both of your portfolios. You have to build a good portfolio to get modeling jobs, you see."

Jill thought modeling was beginning to sound complicated. Why couldn't the agency just find the jobs for me? she wondered.

Alison flipped through Jill's photos from *Fashion Miss.* "I'm sure you can use some of these for your model's book. That's what we call a portfolio of your photographs. But you'll need some work by other photographers, too. You'll be on the testing board for several weeks before you start on go-sees."

"Go-sees?" Jill asked. She felt as though she needed an interpreter.

"Those are your interviews with clients to try to get modeling jobs. You go and the client sees what you look like and looks through your book. We'll send you along with another model at first before you start your own go-sees."

"Do beginning models have a lot of go-sees?" Jill asked.

"All day, every day at first," Alison said with a smile. "It's great for your waistline because you do so much walking. And speaking of that, let's get all your measurements and weight."

Jill was aghast when she stepped on the scales. A hundred and seventeen! She'd gained two pounds since coming to New York. "We want you to lose at least five pounds," Alison said. "Will that be any problem for you, Jill?"

"No, I can do it," Jill said confidently. Good-bye bagels, ice cream, candy bars, and French fries, she thought. But it would be worth it, she was sure.

"Start dieting right away," Alison advised. "You want to look your best next week when you're being photographed. We'll talk more when you come in next Monday. Be ready to work fulltime for the next few weeks. It's hard work getting started in this business!"

The staff at *Fashion Miss* was excited that Jill had been accepted by a good agency. She was swamped with congratulations.

"I knew you'd make it!" Katie said as she gave Jill a big hug. "This calls for a celebration. We're taking you to lunch."

Natalie, Katie, and several other staff members treated Jill and her mother to lunch at a famous French restaurant. Jill had a special French salad called *salade nicoise*. She liked it except for the anchovies on top.

Natalie proposed a toast to Jill. "To our latest discovery and the newest Face of the Future . . . the next star on the junior fashion modeling horizon—Jill Larson!"

Six

JILL and her mother spent all day Saturday finding a new place to live. "We can't take taxis all the time anymore," Mrs. Larson told Jill. "We're on a budget now, and we'll just have to get used to the bus system."

"Can we afford to stay in New York, Mom?" Jill asked.

"The agency is giving us an advance to live on while you get started," her mother replied. "And we have some savings . . . I'm sure you'll be getting jobs before too long."

"But what will happen when this month is over?" Jill hated the uncertainty of their situation. "What about Dad? He can't leave his real estate agency."

"Let's just take this one step at a time, Jill," Mrs. Larson answered. "First, we find a place to live, then we get you established in modeling. We'll have to talk to Dad about this, too. Maybe we'll all live here in New York."

Jill couldn't imagine her father leaving his

business in Alderwood for New York City. He'd lived in Alderwood most of his life. "He's stuck there," Jill told herself. "But I'm not stuck. I'm young enough to break free."

It was an exhausting search for a decent place to stay that didn't cost a fortune. Most hotels cost too much. Most apartments required a one-year lease. Finally they settled for an efficiency apartment in a residence hotel. They had one room, a living room-bedroom combination with a tiny kitchenette at one end.

"It's only for a month," Mrs. Larson said. "I'm sure we can make do for now." She paid for a month's rent in advance, and they headed back to their hotel to pack.

"Ooh, Mom, let's stop at that deli," Jill said. "I'm starved for a hamburger and some fries."

"Jill, remember your diet," her mother warned. "You'd better have a chef's salad and a diet drink."

I'll turn into a rabbit with all this lettuce, Jill thought dismally. Pretty soon my nose will begin to twitch. She ate her salad meekly though. She didn't want to look fat in her test photos.

That night Jill called her best friend, Becky, at home in Alderwood. "Beck? It's me, calling from the Big Apple!"

"Jill! It's great to hear your voice," Becky

said. "What's this I hear from Steve about you staying longer in New York?"

"It's true! We're going to stay for a month to see if I can get started in modeling. I got accepted by a good agency." Jill tried to sound calm, but she couldn't keep the excitement out of her voice.

"Wow, a whole month," Becky said. "I'll really miss you. What about school?"

"I guess I'll try to keep up with my assignments," Jill said. "Mom said something about getting me a tutor."

"Steve's going to be pretty upset about this," Becky said. "You'll miss the rest of basketball season. And I guess you'll have to resign from the school play."

Basketball? School play? Doesn't she realize where I am? Jill wondered. I'm in *New York,* she wanted to shout, modeling for a top magazine, and seeing plays on Broadway! And Alderwood Junior High just isn't very important anymore.

"I have to go Becky," Jill said. "I'll write to you. Tell everyone my good news!"

The Larsons spent Sunday getting settled in their new apartment. There was no TV and Jill's mother said they didn't need one. "You'll be too busy to watch TV," she said. "You have your homework assignments and your exercises to do, and remember, you have to be

47

asleep early every night."

Jill smashed a pile of clothes in a small dresser drawer angrily. No TV, no long telephone calls, no junk food, no staying up late, she thought. Models had to give up everything!

"I know this is hard, honey," her mom said as she helped Jill unpack. "But just think how you'll feel when you see your face on the cover of *Fashion Miss*. All the sacrifices will be worth it then, believe me."

On Monday morning Jill and her mom met with Alison at the Prestige Agency. Alison handed Jill a large black notebook that zipped shut. It said PRESTIGE in white letters on the cover.

"This is your model's book, Jill," Alison said. "You have some good photos here that *Fashion Miss* has given permission for you to use. And here's your date book. Keep that with you at all times. That's for your daily schedule of go-sees and for your bookings, we hope. Bookings are what we call individual jobs for clients," Alison explained.

She showed them a sheet of paper with several photos of a young model. "This is called a composite. You leave one of these at every go-see and with every photographer you visit. As soon as you get your books built up, we'll help you choose the very best shots.

Then you can have your own composites printed."

"How long will all of this take?" Jill asked. It sounded like a long process. She wanted to model again, to have all those experts helping her look beautiful.

"Oh, it can take several months," Alison said. "But I know you're just here on a trial basis. So we've booked you solid in the next few weeks. You'll be on full-time testing with photographers and then go-sees. You'll be a busy young lady, Jill."

Alison slid typed agendas across the table to Jill and her mother. "Here's your schedule for this week. And here's a map. You'll be doing a lot of walking and riding buses. Oh, and tomorrow afternoon, you'll be going on go-sees with another young model, Paula Gregory. She's a high school student in Connecticut and she commutes to the city."

Mrs. Larson went into another office to call the hospital where she worked to ask for an extended leave of absence. She also called Jill's school in Alderwood. Alison took Jill to another office and introduced her to a model named Peggy Marcus.

"Peggy, would you tell Jill about your model's bag?" Alison asked. "Jill's just getting started in modeling, so I'm sure you can give her some tips on what she'll need."

Peggy opened up her large totebag and started taking out the contents. "I have everything in here but the kitchen sink," Peggy said, laughing. "It's hard to know just what you'll need on an assignment, so it's best to be prepared."

Jill was amazed at how much Peggy had crammed in her bag. She saw a makeup kit, brushes, hot rollers, hair dryer, different styles of underwear, pantyhose, jewelry, scarves, a leotard, and two pairs of shoes!

"Isn't that heavy to carry around all day?" Jill asked Peggy.

"It sure is. And don't forget you often have your model's book with you too, depending on your schedule for the day," Peggy said. "It's good exercise though, like walking with weights!"

Mrs. Larson came to get Jill. They thanked Peggy, and then they said good-bye to Alison.

"Don't expect too much at first," Alison warned. "You're just meeting the photographers now. If one or two agree to photograph you this week, that will be great. Be sure to call us twice a day in case anything comes up. Good luck!"

Jill wondered how long it would be before she was really modeling again. All these test photos and go-sees seemed like an awfully slow procedure.

Mrs. Larson was checking Jill's schedule against her map. "We're really going to be running today, Jill," she said. "We see ten photographers today alone!"

They walked to some of Jill's appointments and took the bus to others. It was hard finding their way in a strange big city.

"Be careful," Jill's mom kept warning. "Keep a tight grip on your purse."

Most of the photographers they met with were polite, but not interested in photographing Jill at that time. A few took Jill's name and number and said they would call her when they had more time. One photographer said she'd test Jill after the *Fashion Miss* cover came out.

"Hmmpf," Jill's mom snorted as soon as they left that studio. "After that cover comes out, you won't need to test with anyone. You'll be established then—a cover girl!"

They stopped at some neighborhood shops on their way home to buy food for dinner. Plain fish, plain vegetables, fruit—boring, Jill thought. I have to quit thinking about the food I *want* to eat and start concentrating on what I *have* to eat. Five pounds isn't going to just fall off. She did extra sit-ups and leg-lifts while her mom got dinner ready.

After their simple dinner Jill worked on her homework for a couple of hours. Then she closed her books and wrote a postcard to Steve.

Dear Steve,

Becky has probably told you by now that we're staying in New York for a month. I was accepted by the Prestige Agency, so I really want to give modeling a try.

I really miss seeing you and I hope basketball is going great for you. Have fun till I get back. (But not *too* much fun!)

Love,
Jill

She thought about Steve that night while she was trying to go to sleep. Would he wait for her to come back from New York? Or would he have a new girl friend by then?

Jill's thoughts drifted back again to her wonderful week with *Fashion Miss.* Maybe once she started modeling again, she wouldn't feel Steve was so important. She remembered all the nice editors at *Fashion Miss*, the limousine, the fancy restaurants, and that special grown-up feeling she had in front of the camera. That world could be hers all the time if she stayed in New York.

Maybe it will be a long time before I go back to Alderwood, she thought sleepily. And maybe I'll just have to forget about Steve.

Seven

THE next morning Jill and her mom interviewed with five photographers. And the last one agreed to test photograph Jill. The photographer was a young woman named Eve Riley.

"I think you have a very natural look, Jill," Eve said. "Your career will really take off after your *Fashion Miss* cover comes out." Jill agreed to come back later in the week for her test-photo session.

That afternoon Mrs. Larson began to look for a tutor for Jill. "You can just keep up with your assignments from home for now," Mrs. Larson said. "But I'll be looking into a professional children's school for you later."

"What's that?" Jill wondered.

"Oh, that's a private school for kids who model or act or dance professionally," her mom answered. "Then you can miss school when you need to—in case you're modeling on location in the Bahamas or Europe, for example," she said with a grin.

Jill reported to the modeling agency at two o'clock. There she met a successful model. She was pretty enough, with high cheekbones and long, wavy ash-blonde hair. But she seems so normal, Jill thought, not sophisticated or glamorous at all.

Paula and Jill found lots to talk about on Paula's rounds of go-sees. Paula explained how she had commuted to New York for the past four years to model.

"I usually come in to the city about three days a week now," she said to Jill. "And I work fulltime in the summers. Last year I went to Japan to model for a month."

"Japan?" Jill was amazed that modeling could have taken Paula so far away.

"Oh, yes, the American look is very big there," Paula said. "Prestige takes several girls over every summer. Maybe you can go this year. We had a great time."

Paula and Jill stopped at several advertising agencies to meet art directors. Paula was calm and self-assured as she met prospective clients. She showed everyone her model's book and left her composite.

"How long did it take you to learn how to do all this?" Jill asked. "I'm so nervous meeting all these strangers."

"You do have to have a thick skin," Paula admitted. "Sometimes they talk about you like you're not even there. But you get used to it."

"How often do you have go-sees?"

Paula laughed. "Oh, all the time. It never ends unless you're a supermodel like Brooke Shields or Christie Brinkley. You have to be constantly working on getting your next bookings."

They began a long walk to the next go-see. Jill shivered in the cold despite her wool coat and high boots. Paula told her all about her high school and how she managed to juggle her classes with modeling.

"I can't be in any afterschool activities," Paula said. "And I miss that sometimes. But I go to all the games on the weekends. And I have a boyfriend at my high school."

"I really miss my friends at home," Jill said wistfully. "It's getting kind of boring just being with my mom all the time."

"I have an idea," Paula said. "I have a modeling job on Friday afternoon. Why don't you come along and then you can go home on the train with me for the weekend?"

"That would be great! But I'll have to check with my mom," Jill said. "I'd like that."

"You'll like East Fairfield," Paula said. "It's a little old Connecticut town—very New England. We have a basketball game Friday night, too. I'll have my mom call yours tonight if you want."

They stopped at several photographers' studios to drop off Paula's composites. Then they returned to the agency where Jill was to meet her mother.

Jill introduced her mom to Paula and Paula repeated her invitation. "That sounds wonderful," Mrs. Larson said. "I think I'll visit some old friends who live in New Jersey if you'll be busy, Jill."

"See you on Friday then," Jill said. "Thanks, Paula!"

The next day Jill and her mother woke up to snow. Jill called the agency, but Alison said to keep right on with her appointments. "A couple of inches doesn't stop New York," Alison laughed. "We'd have to stay home half the winter if everything stopped for just a few inches of snow."

So Jill and her mother bundled up in their warmest clothes and set out early for the bus. Jill couldn't believe how cold she was while they waited for the bus. It was never this cold at home, she thought. And the wind!

Their bus was jammed with extra riders when it finally showed up. Jill couldn't find a seat and had to cling to an overhead railing to keep from falling down whenever the bus stopped.

They trudged from one photographer to the next, fighting their way through the snow and ice. "This is horrible, Mom," Jill finally complained. "Let's stop and have some doughnuts and hot chocolate."

"We can't stop, Jill," her mother said. "You have another appointment in half an hour. And hot chocolate is too fattening."

They finally caught a cab to Jill's last appointment of the day. Jill and her mother stood in front of the studio door, wet and shivering.

"Good grief!" the photographer said when he opened the door. "You both look frozen. Come on in. I'm Keith Watson."

Keith let them sit down and warm up. Then he brought them some hot tea. "My shoot this afternoon was cancelled," he said. "So I could do some test photos now if you have time."

"Right now?" Jill asked. "But what—"

"That would be fine, Keith," Jill's mom interrupted. "Wouldn't it, Jill?" She gave Jill one of her pointed looks.

So Jill quickly fixed her hair and applied more makeup. Keith arranged some big lights covered with what looked like white umbrellas. Jill sat on a canvas director's chair while Keith's camera clicked away.

"That's fine, Jill," Keith called out. "Now try standing in front of that gray backdrop."

He had Jill move freely for some action shots. Then he took a series of close-ups and the session was over.

"I can show you the contact sheets as soon as they're developed," Keith said. "Those are tiny prints developed in long strips just to see which photos are best. Then you can decide which one you want for your book."

"You see," said Mrs. Larson as they stepped out into the cold, snowy dusk. "If we'd stayed home today, you would have missed this opportunity for your first test session with a photographer." They took a taxi home to celebrate.

* * * * *

By Friday Jill didn't feel quite like such a beginner any more. She had her test shoot on Friday morning. This time she was more prepared and brought several changes of clothes and all her makeup. The photographer and Jill's mom both thought the photos would be excellent.

"This should give us enough choice in photos to have your composites printed, Jill," Mrs. Larson said. "Then we can really get busy with your go-sees. You'll be on your way!"

Jill found herself looking forward to her

weekend with Paula. Jill loved her mom and appreciated her support. But she missed being with other kids and having fun with her friends.

Jill and Paula met at the agency and then went on to Paula's booking. It was an ad for summer sandals that would run in all the teen fashion magazines.

"This is a good booking," Paula explained. "It might run more than one month in the magazines. That way I'll get more exposure in the field. And maybe the client will have me model for their fall ad, too."

Jill sat quietly in the corner while Paula talked first to the fashion stylist, then the ad agency art director and the photographer. She's so poised, Jill thought, so calm and confident. She knows just what to say to everyone. Can I ever be like that?

Paula finished fixing her own hair and makeup. "You don't very often have a hairstylist or makeup artist on shoots like this," Paula told Jill. "That's why you need all those supplies in your model's bag."

Jill followed Paula into the studio where the others were waiting. Paula had to stand halfway up a stepladder holding a bucket of paint and a paintbrush.

"Hang on to the ladder," the art director said. "And now stick your leg out so the sandal will show. That's it."

For an hour and a half Paula stood on the ladder with her leg held in various positions. The art director and photographer told Paula how to stand and what to do next.

Jill couldn't believe Paula had to stay in that awkward position for such a long time. Wasn't she tired? Jill wondered. And didn't her leg hurt? She asked Paula about it on the train to Connecticut.

"Yes, it was tiring," Paula agreed. "But that's part of the job. Modeling is hard work— harder than people outside of the business realize."

"But couldn't they have given you a rest?" Jill asked.

"Well, you're paid by the hour," Paula explained. "Usually they don't break for several hours." She smiled at Jill. "It wasn't so bad. Wait till you're modeling bathing suits at the beach in December or winter coats in July. Then you'll find out what modeling's really like."

Jill didn't like the sound of those modeling jobs at all. That wasn't glamorous or exciting. That sounded like torture!

Eight

THEIR train pulled into East Fairfield at six o'clock. Paula's father was waiting to drive them home.

"This *is* a pretty town," Jill remarked as they drove past old New England homes and a main street of small shops.

"That's why we don't mind commuting over an hour to New York," Paula's dad said with a smile.

Paula's house was a brick Cape Cod style with a red door and a bay window. Her mother met them at the door. "Welcome, Jill," she said. "I'm Brenda Gregory, Paula's mom."

Jill immediately felt surrounded by the warmth of Paula's home and family. Paula showed her to a pretty yellow and white guest room with a slanted ceiling and lace curtains. Jill thought of her own blue bedroom at home, her canopy bed, and her tape player and tape collection. How far away home seems right now, she thought to herself.

Jill combed her hair and checked her makeup in the small mirror. She hoped she didn't look too young to meet Paula's friends that night. After all, Paula was in tenth grade, so her friends would all be older than Jill.

"Dinner's ready, Jill!" Paula's voice floated up the stairway. Jill hurried down the stairs and turned to go into the dining room.

"Hi. You must be Jill."

Jill looked up into the very handsome face of a guy about her own age, with wavy dark blond hair like Paula's.

"I'm Alex, Paula's brother. Are you hungry?"

"Starved," was all Jill could think of to say. Paula never said she had a brother, Jill thought. And such a cute one at that.

Jill couldn't believe how hungry she felt at the sight of a home-cooked dinner. Roast beef, carrots, mashed potatoes, gravy—she hadn't eaten like that since she left Alderwood. She and her mom ate mostly salads and diet frozen dinners in their efficiency apartment. Their kitchen was too small to do much cooking.

Jill concentrated on the excellent dinner as pleasant conversation flowed around her. Alex was as self-confident as his sister. He told Jill he was a freshman at East Fairfield High.

"I'm going to the game with you and Paula

tonight," Alex said. "You don't want to be stuck with all those older kids by yourself," he joked.

"Why? How old is Troy, Paula?" Jill asked. Paula hadn't told her much about her boyfriend, Troy, yet.

"Oh, he's a junior," Paula said. "He's seventeen."

"Probably be gray like me soon," her dad said, laughing.

Jill turned down Mrs. Gregory's offer of spice cake for dessert. She'd overeaten already as it was. She sipped her hot tea slowly and thought of her own father and brother. Were they having frozen dinners or take-out pizza that night for dinner? She'd almost forgotten how nice it was to have a family dinner in a comfortable home. Didn't her mom miss that? Jill wondered.

Troy picked them all up in his parents' car and they went on to the basketball game. They sat with a big group of kids—Paula, Troy, and Alex knew everyone.

"It's not a huge high school," Alex explained. "That's one of the nice things about East Fairfield."

"Do you like being in high school as a ninth grader?" Jill asked him. "At my school in Washington our ninth grade is still in junior high."

"Well, we are the babies of the school," Alex laughed. "But Paula's friends aren't snobs. They let me tag along."

Jill and Alex turned their attention to the game. They helped cheer East Fairfield to a 60-58 victory. After the game the whole group went out for pizza. Paula and Jill each had diet drinks and only one small slice of pizza each.

"Oh, you models," one of Paula's girl friends said teasingly. "I'm glad *I* can eat six pieces of pizza."

"Remember, you are what you eat!" Troy cracked back.

Jill felt relaxed and happy, happier than she'd felt in quite a while. These kids accepted her as an equal right away, even though she was younger. Maybe becoming a model had helped her in that respect.

She began to think of her friends at home in Alderwood. Had they gone to a game and out for pizza, too? She wasn't even sure how her brother was doing on the basketball team. Probably Steve had gone to the game . . . but with the guys? Jill wondered. Or with another girl?

The next day Jill and Paula went shopping in the little shops in East Fairfield. Jill bought a pewter bracelet for her mother.

"It's so calm and nice here," Jill told Paula.

"So different from the city."

Paula smiled. "I couldn't live there myself. As they say, 'It's a nice place to visit, but I wouldn't want to live there!' That's true for me. I wouldn't leave East Fairfield until it's time for college."

Jill and Paula walked back to the Gregory's house and played backgammon with Paula's father until it was time to help fix dinner. Jill stuffed herself again on Mrs. Gregory's delicious cooking.

After dinner Troy, Paula, Alex, and Jill walked downtown to the movie theater to see a new science fiction film. Jill told Alex all about Alderwood on the way to the movie. Once or twice she thought about Steve and wondered what he was doing and if he was having fun without her.

On the way home Alex took Jill's hand firmly. "It's getting icy," he said. "It's supposed to snow tonight, you know. Maybe you'll get snowed in and you won't be able to leave."

"I'd like that," Jill said with a smile. "It's nice staying with your family."

"You'll have to come back then," Alex said, and gave Jill's hand a squeeze.

The next morning Jill woke early and looked out her window to a sparkling white world of snow and ice.

"Jill!" Paula called as she knocked on the door. "Wake up! Breakfast is in fifteen minutes and then we're going sledding!"

Jill dressed quickly in wool pants and a warm sweater. After a breakfast of pancakes and real New England maple syrup, they all bundled up in parkas, boots, hats, and mittens. Mr Gregory and Alex tied a sled and a toboggan to the top of their station wagon.

"We're going to the golf course, Jill," Mrs. Gregory explained. "It's the best sledding around here."

Although she was a good skier, Jill had only been sledding a couple of times before. And she'd never been on a big toboggan. Alex explained how she had to hold on to the person in front with her arms and keep her feet and legs tucked in.

"Don't worry," Mr. Gregory said cheerfully. "I'm steering up here. Haven't hit a tree yet!"

They flew down a steep hill with fresh snow flying up in their faces. Jill loved the clean whiteness of the new snow on the rolling hills. She went down the hill on the toboggan again and again, feeling her muscles warm up with the exercise.

"Having fun?" Alex asked. "Your cheeks are all pink."

"It's wonderful!" Jill said enthusiastically. "It's almost as much fun as skiing. I'd do this all winter if I lived here."

Finally they were too exhausted to drag the toboggan up the hill one more time, and they headed home. After drinking cups of steaming hot chocolate, the whole Gregory family took Jill to the station.

"Thank you *so* much," Jill said. "It was a super weekend!"

The Gregorys stood on the platform and waved at Jill as her train pulled out. She stared out the window as Connecticut towns rolled by. She thought of the warmth of home and her mom's regular cooking, her dad coming home from his office, her brother from the basketball court. She thought of play practice and talking on the phone with Becky every night. And she thought about Steve.

When her train pulled in to the station in New York, Jill saw her mom standing all alone on the platform. She was clutching her purse tightly, looking around warily. The sight brought tears to Jill's eyes.

New York can never be home, Jill thought. There's no trees, no hills, no mountains. Why, Alderwood doesn't even have a train station!

"Hi, sweetheart!" Jill's mom called out. "I didn't see you at first. Great news! The agency called this morning. You have your first booking—tomorrow!"

"Tomorrow!" Jill gasped. "But I haven't

even been on any go-sees yet."

"This is through the art director who worked with your friend Paula last Friday," her mother explained. "He needs someone in a hurry for tomorrow morning and he thought of you."

"What kind of job is it?" Jill asked.

"I'm not sure," Mrs. Larson said. "Some kind of ad, I think. The agency will call you tonight. I made crabmeat salad for our dinner to celebrate."

"Another salad," Jill groaned to herself. "It's back to reality and my diet."

Her mother chattered all the way home about the friends she had visited in New Jersey. "I showed them all your pictures," she said. "And they all thought you were so pretty." She talked on and on about Jill's career. Jill only half-listened as she stared out at the dirty gray snow from the bus window.

Finally as they took the elevator to their apartment, Jill's mom asked, "By the way, how was Connecticut?"

"Wonderful," Jill said, with a fleeting memory of the sun sparkling on fresh snow. "Just wonderful. Nothing at all like New York City."

Nine

JILL tried hard not to be nervous the next morning on the way to her real booking. Her hair was perfect. Her nails were freshly manicured. Her makeup expertly applied. She wore one of her new outfits and felt she really looked like a model now.

Too bad I didn't look like this all the time at home, Jill thought. But I didn't have so much time to spend on my appearance then. It takes hours to look like this.

"You look just perfect, Jill," her mom said as they entered the photographer's studio. "You look like a real pro!"

They met with the photographer and the art director who explained the assignment. Jill would be the model for an ad for stuffed animals for Easter.

"Stuffed *toys*?" Jill couldn't believe it. "Don't you want a little girl for that?"

"Jill!" her mother said in a shocked tone.

"I'm sure they know who they want."

"You see, this ad is for the major women's magazines," the art director explained. "The copy will say something like, 'She's not too old for the Easter bunny.' And you'll be holding this big pink stuffed bunny."

Jill hated the idea. She had tried so hard to look a little older and more sophisticated. And now her first job was holding a stuffed bunny!

She was given a fuzzy white sweater to wear and a pink ribbon for her hair. A hair ribbon, she thought in disgust. This really is too much. It's a good thing my hair isn't long anymore or they'd want it in pigtails.

The art director asked Jill to remove most of her eye makeup. "Nothing too grown-up for this ad," he said. "And just a touch of pink lip gloss. We want the girl-next-door look here."

Jill sat on a bench surrounded by all sorts of stuffed animals—chicks, ducks, bears, bunnies, and lambs. She held the big pink bunny on her lap.

I'll look like I'm eight years old, she thought. This isn't what my career is supposed to be like at all. She threw her mother a pleading look, but her mom just smiled and gave her the thumbs-up sign.

Oh, please, Jill thought. I think I'm going to be sick. But she smiled sweetly and hugged her bunny.

I hope no one at home sees this ad. I'll never hear the end of it, she thought.

Jill smiled her way through an hour of photos with the bunny. She found being photographed with stuffed animals pretty boring, but at least it was a fairly short job.

The art director asked for a few more shots and then said they had enough film. "Thanks, Jill," he said as he gave her the pay voucher to turn in to the modeling agency. "We'll send the proofs to Prestige."

That's it? Jill wondered. No one even said I did a good job. She had expected more encouragement from her first real modeling job.

"They didn't compliment me or anything, Mom," Jill complained on their way out of the studio.

"That's because you're a professional now," her mother tried to explain. "You looked so darling up there, honey. I know it'll be a great ad. Your dad will just love it."

I'm sure he will, Jill thought, because I'll look like a little girl. When her father called that night she told him about her first booking.

"Well, I think it sounds nice, Jill," he said. "I'm glad you're doing something wholesome instead of posing in one of those weird New York fashion get-ups."

"But it's not what I want, Dad," Jill said. "In

fact . . . I'm not sure New York is what I want."

After a little pause her father said, "Jill, you know my opinion on that. I wish you'd come home tomorrow. Your brother and I miss you and your mom, too."

"But I don't want to miss my chance at a career," Jill said.

Her dad chuckled. "You're only thirteen, Jill. You've got all the time in the world for a career, for several different careers in fact. And New York will always be there. You can go back again when you're older."

"But this is my big chance now, Dad," Jill protested. "When my face is on the cover of *Fashion Miss* it will show that I'm the newest model in town."

"You can always go for it again later," her dad said firmly, "if you want it enough."

That night Jill thought about what her dad had said. Maybe she could come back to New York, after high school or college. Then she could come by herself and live with other models in an apartment. That might be more fun.

Jill and her mother met with Alison at the agency the next morning to select the photos for her composite. Jill wanted to use the photos that made her seem older. But Alison explained that Jill had to be able to look younger or older. "That's the key to a really successful model," she said. "A versatile face."

They finally selected five photos for the composite. Jill thought she looked too young in most of them, but she listened to Alison's advice.

"We'll have these printed up for you today," Alison said. "You can pick them up tomorrow. Oh, we can have your prints ready for your book, too. Then you'll have everything you need for your go-sees."

That week was a confusing blur of one studio or office after another for Jill and her mom. Mrs. Larson kept track of all the scheduling and Jill just went along and smiled.

Pretty face—but a little too old, a little too young, not quite what we're looking for. Jill kept smiling, but inside she was seething. Don't they know there's a person in here, she wanted to scream. Don't just discuss my pretty face. There's a mind right behind it that's hearing everything you say—and hating it.

Jill tried to remember what Paula had told her about models needing thick skins. She even called Paula one night to talk about it.

"You've got to be relaxed around people talking about you," Paula told Jill. "Don't lose your confidence. That's a model's most important asset."

Jill felt more and more tired as each day

passed. All the walking to go-sees was tiring. She had to get up at six every day to get her hair washed and dried. She had to do her exercises and homework every night and make sure her manicure was perfect. She had to meet with her tutor one night each week. There was never any time left over for fun and relaxation.

"We'll try to do some sightseeing this weekend," her mother promised when Jill complained. "And you can catch up on your sleep and your homework, too."

Late Friday afternoon Mrs. Larson checked in with the agency for the last time that week. She came out of the phone booth with a huge smile.

"Great news, Jill! You have an all-day booking on Monday! That should boost your spirts."

"Wow, Mom!" Jill said, smiling. "What kind of booking?"

"It's an ad for some kind of summer clothes," her mother replied. "The agency said it's a 'weather permit' job. That means if it rains or snows, the shoot is cancelled."

"Rains or snows?" Jill said. "You mean this job is outdoors?"

"Right. On location in a park, I think."

"In this weather?" Jill couldn't believe it. "I'll freeze!"

"Oh, don't worry," Mrs. Larson said soothingly. "We'll take some hot tea and you'll probably move around a lot."

But as soon as the shoot started Jill discovered that her worries were well founded. She was to model six different coordinating summer outfits. And the only place to change was in the back of a freezing cold van.

The photographer's assistant spread out carpets of fake grass and put out pots of bright spring flowers. These props were positioned in front of evergreen trees, so it did almost look like spring.

But it doesn't feel like spring, Jill thought as she shivered in the cold. She kept her coat on every minute she could.

"Okay, Jill, hop up on that park bench," the photographer directed. "Come on, look cheerful. You're not cold!"

Jill tried to look happy and warm, as though it wasn't February. At least it isn't snowing, she thought.

"Okay, Jill. Now run around the edge of that big fountain," the photographer ordered. "And look like you're having fun!" he barked.

He doesn't have to be such a grouch, Jill thought. He's not the one out here in summer shorts and a short top. She climbed up on the edge of the fountain and started to walk around the rim.

"No—run, Jill! Get some motion!"

"What if I fall in?" Jill asked desperately.

"Don't worry," the photographer's assistant said with a trace of sarcasm. "There isn't any water in there in the winter."

So Jill dutifully ran around the empty fountain, trying to look like she was having fun. Her throat and her head were hurting and it was getting harder to keep smiling.

"Okay, half hour break for lunch," the photographer called. "There's a deli across the street."

Jill ordered potato soup and hot chocolate. "I need something hot and filling, Mom," Jill said when she saw her mother's disapproving look.

"You could have hot tea," Mrs. Larson said quietly. "Hot chocolate is very fattening."

"Give me a break, will you?" Jill said flatly. She felt too tired and sick to argue. "I think I must be coming down with something."

After their lunch break Jill changed into pants and matching sweatshirt. "At least this is a little warmer," she told the stylist. This time Jill had to run around the fountain again and then jump off the park bench. Art directors sure are big on action shots, Jill thought.

"Okay, Jill, now we want you up in this tree," the photographer called out.

"Are they trying to torture me or what?" Jill mumbled to herself. The photographer's assistant lifted Jill up so she could swing by her hands from a low branch.

"Okay, now kick your legs and smile, Jill!" the art director yelled, "No, a big smile!"

Again and again Jill dangled from the tree, trying to look like she was enjoying herself.

"Mom, I just feel awful," Jill said when she was finally given a short break. "How much longer do you think this will take?"

"Not too much longer, honey," her mother answered. "I think you just have one more outfit."

The last outfit was a bathing suit with matching cover-up and shirt. They were all done in a bright print that picked up the colors of the other outfits. Jill thought she would have enjoyed modeling that outfit if she'd been indoors or somewhere where the weather was sunny and warm.

She stood shivering in the cold, holding open the cover-up to show off the bathing suit. "This is just ridiculous," Jill finally admitted to herself. She had to clench her teeth to keep them from chattering.

"This outfit looks good," the art director said to the photographer. "She's not too thin for it. Hope her legs don't photograph too heavy."

Jill stared at the art director in amazement. Was he talking about *her*? After all her dieting and exercising, someone still thought she weighed too much. Jill had to fight to keep from crying. She was so cold and tired. "Where's all the glamour modeling is supposed to have," she asked herself. "Right now I just feel sick . . . sick of the whole modeling business."

By the time they got back to the apartment Jill was sneezing and her throat felt like sandpaper. "I feel terrible," Jill told her mother. "All I want is a great big glass of orange juice. Then I'm going right to bed."

"I'm afraid there isn't any orange juice," her mother said as she looked through their mail. "How about some tea?"

"No orange juice!" Jill snapped. "We *always* had orange juice in the freezer at home."

"Well, your dad does the shopping there," her mother said calmly. "He's better at keeping things in stock than I am. Here's a letter for you from home. Maybe that will cheer you up."

Jill recognized Steve's handwriting on the envelope. She hadn't had time to write him much lately. She decided to answer this letter right away or maybe even call Steve. Jill ripped open the envelope and flopped down on the sofa-bed to read Steve's letter.

Dear Jill,

I guess you know I'm not too happy about my girl friend living in New York. I thought you would care enough about your friends to come back home.

When and if you come back to Alderwood we can talk about our relationship . . . if you still care. Until then I'm taking out other girls.

Good luck with your modeling career. I hope it's worth it.

Steve

Ten

"JILL, come on!" her mother called. "It's six-fifteen. Time to get up."

"Ugh," Jill moaned. "I can't get up. I'm too sick."

"Well, get up and have your shower and then you'll feel better." Mrs. Larson shook Jill's shoulder. "Come on, you have to wash your hair. You have that important go-see at nine."

"Didn't you hear me coughing and sneezing last night? I'm sick. S-I-C-K, get it? I'm not going anywhere today."

"But if you miss this go-see you'll lose the booking for sure," her mother said. "Can't you pull yourself together just for this morning?"

"No," Jill said flatly. "I'm going back to sleep. And I'd really like some orange juice." She pulled the covers halfway over her head.

I can't believe this is my mother, she thought as she relaxed again under the warmth of the blankets. Mom used to make me stay home from school whenever I had a bad cold at home. And now she wants me to get all dressed up and smile and look pretty just for a go-see. She'd probably drag me off my deathbed if she thought it would lead to a modeling job, Jill thought grimly.

Jill awakened several hours later when she heard her mother come in from outside. "Here's your juice, Jill," Mrs. Larson said. "And I got you some cold tablets, too. That should help."

"How about some homemade potato soup for lunch?" Jill asked. "And some rice pudding?"

"Oh, those are pretty fattening foods, Jill," her mother warned. "Can't forget your diet just because you aren't feeling well."

"But that's what you always made me at home when I was sick!" Jill protested.

"We aren't at home now," her mother said tightly.

"I know!" Jill yelled as she stomped into the bathroom. "And I wish we were! At least I'd get a little sympathy there."

Jill stayed in bed for two days with her cold. The agency cancelled all her go-sees for the rest of that week to give her time to recover. Jill got all caught up in her homework and met with her tutor. She even had time to read the latest fashion magazines.

On Friday Alex called Jill. He was very sympathetic about her cold. "I know how it is," he said. "I catch every kind of cold and flu they invent."

"I'm feeling better now," Jill admitted. "I should be okay by Monday."

"Save your strength for next weekend," Alex said. "We're having our winter homecoming game and dance on Saturday and I'd like you to come."

"Oh, Alex, that would be great," Jill said. She would love to get out of New York and visit the Gregorys again.

"You can come out with Paula on Friday again and stay for the whole weekend," Alex offered. "We all enjoyed your stay with us last time."

"I did too," Jill said.

"I'll call you later this week with the details," Alex said. Take care of yourself now. Bye."

"Mom!" Jill said as soon as she put down the phone. "I'm invited to East Fairfield next weekend for a homecoming game and dance. Alex just called."

"Not *next* Saturday night?" her mother said.

"Yes, why?"

"I was just going to tell you when you got that call," Mrs. Larson explained. "The agency phoned today while you were napping. We're invited to a big party that night given by the owner of the agency, Garrison Westcott. Alison said it's an honor to be invited. I've already accepted for us."

"But, Mom!" Jill wailed. "Can't you go ahead without me?"

"Of course not!" her mother laughed. "It's you they want to see, silly. I'm just the chaperone. But I'll tell you a little secret. Mr. Westcott's son saw your composite and he wants to meet you."

"What does he do—pick his girl friends from the agency photos?" Jill suggested. She disliked him already.

"Now calm down," Mrs. Larson said smoothingly. "There will be other weekends with your friends. But Mr. Westcott only has these big parties twice a year, Alison said. And they're very important. Lots of photographers and ad agency people will be there. It's important for your career."

"Career, career," Jill grumbled. "That's all I hear these days."

"Well, that has to come first now," her mother said. "You're a professional now, don't forget."

"That's just the trouble," Jill said to herself. "Sometimes I'd like to forget it."

* * * * *

Jill and her mom sat in icy silence on the way to Garrison Westcott's party. Jill had been mad at her mother all week for making her cancel her plans with Alex. And Jill's mom was mad at Jill for being mad. The walls of the tiny apartment had seemed to close in on their anger all week long.

"I'm sick of it," Jill told herself. They had had another whole week of go-sees without a single booking. "I'm tired of smiling at strangers and having them talk about my looks in front of me. I'm sick of living in a little shoe box apartment when we have a nice big house at home. I'm tired of doing exercises and dieting and washing my hair every morning at six o'clock. And I'm tired of trying to do my homework with only a tutor once a week to help me. I miss Dad and Chris and Becky and . . . Jill bit her lip to keep the tears back." She didn't want her mother to see her cry.

The taxi stopped in front of a huge, elegant apartment building. A uniformed doorman met them and took their invitation. A silent elevator whisked them to the penthouse at the top of the building.

"I hope we're dressed all right," Mrs. Larson said in the elevator.

Jill looked at her mother in surprise. "You look lovely," Jill said. Her mother was always poised and confident, and she did look charming that night in a red wool suit.

"So do you, honey," Mrs. Larson said, and squeezed Jill's arm. "Let's try to put our disagreement behind us and have a good time."

A butler took their coats in the large entry hall of the penthouse. Jill tried not to stare too much as they entered the living room where the party was in progress. She'd never seen a home like this before.

Two walls of the room were windows, looking out on a spectacular view of New York at night. French doors opened onto a large terrace with a hot tub, a fountain, and real trees.

The living room was all in white, with white leather sofas and chairs. There was even a white grand piano.

It's all so huge, Jill thought is awe. This room is about the size of our whole house at home.

They stopped at one of the buffet tables piled high with fruit, salads, caviar, and tiny sandwiches. On one table was a centerpiece of ice carved in the shape of birds. Another table had vegetables and fruit carved to look like a Viking ship.

"Ah, here you are," Alison said from behind Jill. "And here's your host. You remember Jill Larson and her mother, don't you, Garrison?

Jill is one of our rising stars."

"Of course," Mr. Westcott smiled at them smoothly. "Welcome to you both. My son wants to meet you, Jill. He's been bewitched by your photos."

Jill smiled blankly. This can't be real, she thought. What am I doing here?

Mr. Westcott took her arm and steered her over to one of the white leather sofas. "Trip, here's that young lady you've been dying to meet," Mr. Westcott said. "Jill Larson, my son, Garrison Westcott III. Trip for short."

"Jill!" Trip said, as he grabbed both of her hands in his. "I've been waiting for you."

"You two get acquainted then," said his father. "I'll introduce Mrs. Larson to everyone."

"Your photo doesn't do you justice, Jill," Trip said. "You're much prettier in person."

Jill smiled politely at Trip and sat down next to him. "He *is* Mr. Westcott's son," she told herself. "I guess I'd better be nice to him."

"Trip is an unusual nickname," she said. "I've never heard it before."

"You're kidding!" Trip laughed. "It's really quite common. It's because I'm the third. You know—triple."

"Oh, I see," Jill said. At least he didn't get his nickname from being clumsy. Trip was good-looking, she decided, with clean-cut, preppy looks. But he dressed in that strange, overdone, New York sort of style.

"You're not from around here, are you?" Trip asked as he handed Jill a soft drink in a crystal glass.

"No, I'm from Washington," Jill answered.

"Oh, D.C.," Trip said, nodding. "Is your father in the government?"

"No, not Washington, D.C.," Jill said with a smile. "Washington State, near Seattle."

"Oh, boo! Where it rains all the time?" Trip smiled in a teasing way.

"It's not so bad," Jill answered. "You forget about the rain on sunny days when you can see the snow up on the mountains. And I don't think too much of New York's snow and ice."

"How would you like to escape for a week in the sun?" Trip leaned closer to Jill and put his arm on the back of the sofa.

"Oh, I'd love it," Jill sighed. "But we can't afford any vacations now."

"But you'd be my guest," Trip said smoothly. "We have a condo in St. Thomas. I'm going down for my winter break in three weeks. And I want you to come with me." He put his arm around Jill's shoulder and kissed her neck. "You're just the spring tonic I need."

"Stop it!" Jill jumped up, spilling her drink all over her pale blue dress. "I don't even know you!"

"You know everything about me you need to know," Trip said with a grin. "My dad's the owner of Prestige, don't forget. I could be a good friend to you."

"Friends like you I don't need," Jill said sharply. She turned away and went to find her coat.

After Jill found their coats she looked for her mother. "Jill, what happened?" her mom asked anxiously when she saw the stain on Jill's dress and the look on her face.

"You can stay here if you want to," Jill said as she put on her coat. "But I'm going home—where I belong."

Eleven

"NOW what do you mean about going home?" Mrs. Larson said as soon as they were settled in a taxi.

"You remember home, Mom," Jill said as she stared out the taxi window at the bright lights. ". . .Alderwood, Dad, Chris, our *friends.* I've had it with New York." She explained about Mr. Westcott's son.

"Oh, Jill, he's just a spoiled kid trying to impress you," her mother said calmly. "Don't overreact. You've hardly given modeling a chance yet. Now you've had two bookings already. And as soon as that *Fashion Miss* cover comes out this summer, you're going to be one of the hottest models in New York!"

"But I don't want to wait till then!" Jill glared at her mother. "Don't you ever think about what *I* want? I miss Dad, Chris, Steve, my friends, and school. I want to go home!"

"But Jill, think of the opportunities you'll be

giving up," her mother argued. "There are thousands of girls who would love to be in your shoes. Why, with the start we've made here and your looks—"

"I'm not just another pretty face, Mom!" Jill cried. "I'm a person first! And I'm tired of all this beauty stuff and having people talk about my looks in front of me. I'm tired of always smiling and trying to be polite and charming. I want to go home and wear my old jeans and sit on my own bed in my own room in my own house. . . ." Jill burst into tears and turned away from her mother.

"Oh, sweetie," Jill's mom said as she tried to put her arm around Jill.

"Don't touch me!" Jill cried. "You don't even care what I want. It's only what you want that counts." She refused to talk to her mother anymore that night. Jill fell into bed exhausted and slept till ten the next morning.

When Jill woke up her mother was gone. She had left a note saying, "Gone to pick up paper and fresh bagels. Back soon."

Jill picked up the telephone and dialed her home phone number. "Please be there, Dad," she whispered. "I really need you now."

"Hello?"

"Chris? It's Jill."

"Well, hey, stranger," her brother said. "I thought you'd forgotten us or gone to model in

Paris or something. How's it going?"

"Not very well," Jill said softly. "I want to come home and Mom wants me to stay."

"Aw, come on home," Chris said. "Dad and I are tired of being bachelors. Here, Dad wants to talk to you."

"Jill? Are you coming home?" Jill could hear the love and concern in her father's voice.

"I want to come home," Jill said. "But Mom thinks I haven't given modeling enough of a chance."

"Enough is enough," her father said. "Put your mother on the phone."

"She's not here, Dad," Jill said. "She'll be back in a little while."

"Well, if you've had enough of New York, you're coming home," her dad said. "Tell your mother I'll call her later. And I'll make your return reservations myself—day after tomorrow, okay? That should give you time to settle things there."

"That would be fine," Jill said quietly. A wave of relief washed over her.

"I always thought your staying in New York was a bunch of bunk. But now, at least you know what modeling is all about. It'll be great to have my little girl back again."

"I'll talk to you later then," Jill said. "Thanks, Daddy." She hung up the phone and laid back down on the sofa bed. Only two more days and she'd be home! she thought. Jill got out all her school books and started reading an English assignment. She didn't want to be too far behind when she went back to junior high.

"Oh, hi, honey." Jill's mother hurried in with a bag of groceries and the huge Sunday *New York Times*. "How about a fresh bagel?"

"We won't be able to get bagels like this at home, I guess," Jill said as she bit into one.

"We need to talk about that, Jill." Her mother poured some orange juice. "We'll just take things a little slower from now on. We won't do so many go-sees and you can—"

"No." Jill put down her bagel and faced her mother. "We're going home . . . on Tuesday. I already called Dad and he's making our reservations."

"Just like that, you're giving it all up?" Her mother's voice was bitter.

"It's nothing great to give up, Mom. Can't you see that? Modeling isn't fun like I thought it would be. It's a job, and I'm just not ready for that kind of responsibility yet."

"You could be if you tried!" Her mother's lips were pressed into a thin line.

"But I don't *want* to try anymore!" Jill cried. "You're the one who wants it! And I'm the one who has to hang from a tree in the freezing cold and keep smiling!" She jumped up and ran into the bathroom. When Jill came out her mother was gone.

* * * * *

Jill and her mother spent the evening discussing returning to Alderwood. Finally Mrs. Larson agreed with Jill that it was time to go home. Jill called Paula and Alex to say goodbye, and they promised to keep in touch. Jill invited them to visit her in Alderwood next summer. She felt sad that she wouldn't be able to see them before she left.

On Monday Jill and Mrs. Larson went to the Prestige Agency to meet with Alison.

"I'm very disappointed that you're leaving, Jill," Alison said. "You've made a promising start in a short time. But we do understand that modeling isn't for everyone."

"Thank you," Jill said. "I-I'm sorry I can't stay."

"You may want to come back and try again in a couple of years," Alison offered. "Come back later and try it for a summer."

"Maybe," Jill said. "I'll keep it in mind."

When they left the agency Jill felt a wonderful sense of freedom. Tomorrow she'd be home, back where she belonged!

"Let's go see the Statue of Liberty, Mom. We haven't done that yet." They spent the afternoon as tourists, riding the ferry boats and viewing the great statue.

What a perfect way to end my stay here, Jill thought as she gazed up at the nation's symbol of hope and freedom. Now I'm free, too—free to go home and be myself.

*　*　*　*　*

Jill's mother was unusually quiet on the flight home. Finally she turned to Jill and said, "I guess I owe you an apology, Jill. I did push you a little too hard to stay in New York and try modeling. But I just wanted you to have the strong kind of support from your mother that I never had. I'm sorry if I went a little overboard."

"It's okay, Mom," Jill said, smiling. "I'm not sorry we stayed. I learned a lot about modeling." And about myself, too, she thought.

"Will you be glad to get back to school and your friends?" her mother asked.

"Will I ever! I can't wait for everything to be normal again, the way things used to be."

The weather in Seattle was clear and sunny as they approached the airport. "Mom, look at the mountains!" Jill cried, gazing out at the snow-capped peaks of the Cascade Mountains. "I'm so glad we're home," she whispered.

Jill's father and brother were waiting for the flight. As soon as she entered the airport lobby, Jill was swept up into her dad's big bear hug.

"Jill! I'm so glad you're home!" he said. Jill looked past his shoulder and saw Becky and some of her other friends from school.

"Hi, Becky!" Jill called out and ran over to hug her friend. "It's great to see all of you."

"Welcome back to reality," Becky said. "I brought all your homework assignments with me!"

Jill chattered away with her friends about her stay in New York and what she had missed at school. Then they all went down to the baggage pick-up area to wait for the luggage to arrive.

Jill was talking to her brother when she felt someone staring at her. She looked over and saw Steve leaning against the wall. Jill took a deep breath and walked over to meet him.

"Hi, Steve," Jill said shyly. "Why didn't you come over and talk to us?"

"Oh, I was waiting for all the excitement to die down a little," he said. "And I wanted to see if you'd turned into some kind of movie star."

"I haven't changed much," Jill said. "I just had to find out how much I like it here. I really missed home . . . and my friends."

"You didn't start going out with some handsome male model?" Steve asked, teasing her.

"Are you kidding?" Jill laughed. "I never even met anyone like that. And I had to go to bed at nine every night so I could get up at six to get ready. We didn't even have a TV!"

"Doesn't sound like such a wonderful life to me," Steve said with a smile.

"Modeling is really hard work," Jill said. "A lot harder than I thought it would be."

"Did you bring back any of the pictures from your modeling jobs?" Steve asked.

"Oh, sure, I have a whole portfolio full of them. But they're just souvenirs now."

"Could I have one?" Steve asked. "I'd like to have a picture of my girl friend when she was a famous New York model."

Jill looked at Steve in surprise. "Does that mean. . . ?"

"I'm sorry I got so mad at you for staying in New York," he said. "I guess I was worried you'd never come back."

"I could never stay there," Jill said. "In New York I was just another pretty face."

"You know you're more than that to us," Steve said, "to the people who love you." He took Jill's hand and together they went over to rejoin her family and friends.